WOKE

A YOUNG POET'S CALL TO JUSTICE

MAHOGANY L. BROWNE

WITH **ELIZABETH ACEVEDO** AND **OLIVIA GATWOOD**

ILLUSTRATED BY
THEODORE TAYLOR III

FOREWORD BY
JASON REYNOLDS

Roaring Brook Press

New York

CONTENTS

I grew up in a house
in a family where
my mother allowed me to

talk back talk back
she said   talk back

(you really gon' let that boy talk back?)

just know not to disrespect me
I'm still your mother but know that no ain't
just no and if you want to

talk back talk back

but I ain't gonna hear you
unless you say it like you mean it
and to mean it don't mean it
gotta be said mean

I'm still your mother remember that
you still a human remember that

so stand up straight
lock your shoulders
open your chest
and say your human things so I can hear
you 'cross the room

'cross the world
over all this noise.

Woke: A Young Poet's Call to Justice is, in book form, exactly what my mother meant. It's a collection of proclamations, megaphoning to the young world that they are human and therefore have the right—I'd even go so far as to say the obligation—to talk back, to speak up, to connect with the fortifying elements outside of them, as well as those that exist within. Mahogany L. Browne, Elizabeth Acevedo, and Olivia Gatwood are, together, beacons shining light on prejudice, resistance, self-acceptance, friendship, intersectionality, and inclusion. They are also serving as beacon builders—each of the poems acting as blocks strengthening and heightening every young lighthouse that reads them. Nothing is heavy-handed here, because Browne, Acevedo, and Gatwood clearly understand that soft-handedness works better. Hugs. Handshakes. The ladling of shared soup. Handclaps. Finger snaps. A wave goodbye. Peace signs. Fists in the air in solidarity. Palms reaching up for what's clearly an attainable sky.

Justice looks like many things. To my mother, to me, it was often the freedom to talk back. The freedom to own my voice. What *Woke* knows is that to the future poets—and by poets I mean YOU—it will look like those things and also much, much more.

—Jason Reynolds

WHAT DOES IT MEAN TO BE WOKE?

In the simplest sense, it means to be aware. It means to see your surroundings and challenge how we strengthen our relationships with the government, the community, and nature. To be WOKE is to fight for your civil rights and to fight for the rights of your neighbors. I remember when I first heard neo-soul singer, DJ, and poet Erykah Badu singing "Master Teacher." Throughout the song, the chorus echoed "I stay woke." This refrain was tapping into the energy and curiosity that was introduced with the definition of WOKE during the civil rights movement of the 1960s and the black power movement of the 1970s. The idea of being aware of your surroundings, especially in a time when we are taught to be quiet and not rock the boat, can be difficult to embrace, but this is where our freedom begins.

The idea of WOKE resurfaced with a vengeance in 2016, as a new generation fought for social justice and community accountability. In the spring of 2019, I did a reading for a pre-K class in Bed-Stuy, Brooklyn, and afterward a four-year-old told me WOKE is "to have your eyes wide open, seeing everything." I smiled so big. Only four years old and this little girl was already WOKE!

To be WOKE is to understand that equality and justice for some is not equality and justice at all. We must stay alert. We must ask hard questions. We must stand for what is right—even when it is difficult and scary.

The concept of being WOKE has always been a compass for community leaders and members. Light bearers including Maya Angelou, Nikki Giovanni, June Jordan, Cherríe Moraga, Sonia Sanchez, and Nina Simone have used poetry, plays, and essays to challenge people to be WOKE. *Woke: A Young Poet's Call to Justice* follows in the tradition of these heroes. The poems in this collection come from three women writers with varied perspectives of justice. These poems serve both as instruction manuals and anthems, as literary heartbeats and blueprints of survival for young people everywhere. The ideas they tackle are layered and nuanced, but the message is simple:

Don't Sleep.

—Mahogany L. Browne

ACTIVISM, EVERYWHERE
BY MAHOGANY L. BROWNE

Our voice
Is our greatest power

When we stand together
We can speak up against mistreatment

We are saying that we will not be silent about the mistreatment of people
We are saying we will not be silent

We are standing tall and firm because we believe in equity and equality
We are standing tall and firm

We are not yielding or bending because the conversation is uncomfortable
We are not yielding or bending

We understand activism happens online and offline
In the streets picketing
And in the classroom teaching
On the blogs writing
On the internet sharing information

It happens everywhere
It is active
It is energy
It is resisting to be comfortable
When we all have yet to feel safe and free

THE ABILITY TO BE

BY MAHOGANY L. BROWNE

The ways in which our bodies may move against the wind or the water
climb stairs or swing high in a child's park
—both arms in flight,
all on their own is different.

Sometimes we have sight
sometimes we have the sense of smell
sometimes we are working with a different
set of skills altogether.

There is more than one way to exist.
There is more than one way we learn how to speak
with our hands
or our eyes.
There are different tones to evoke a symphony of laughter.

Our fingers and toes
our arms and torsos
each courageous cloud a thunderous declaration
echoing: I Am Here!

Because the smallest things that make us up
are the largest strokes of beauty that color us brilliant!

But the heart
Oh my! How our hearts beat the same.

IN THE NEXT
BY MAHOGANY L. BROWNE

Things should be different
We must keep our eyes on the prize

The prize is a good life
The good life smells like true freedom
True freedom is a song we should all be able to sing

It will happen in the hills of Appalachia
It will happen in the streets of Brooklyn
It will happen in the veins of Detroit

Discrimination will no longer be tolerated
Hate will have nowhere to hide

Powerful and meek
Strong and brilliant
All of us combined, as one

This is when the sky will break open its blue blue wings
And we will celebrate its lush song

THE GOOD BODY
BY ELIZABETH ACEVEDO

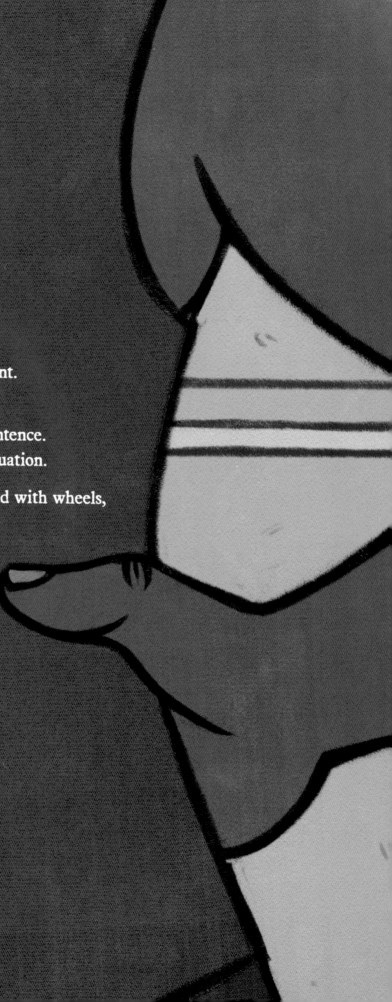

You know your joints
that bend and straighten?

Your mouth and ears and eyes,
your limbs that lengthen

as you reach for the earth or clouds?
You know your hair that maybe coils

upward, stretching, or falls
straight down your back?

Your body can be a jungle gym of movement.
Your body can be a chapel of quietude.

Your body can roll and grow like a long sentence.
Your body can be like small, mighty punctuation.

Your body can be encased in metal, adorned with wheels,
it can need medicine and extra support.

Sometimes, your body can make you angry
or sad;

because it doesn't look how you want it to,
or it doesn't do what you'd like it to;

because it might have limits
that you want to move beyond,

but remember, even on the days
you aren't feeling yourself:

Your body is always a good body
because it carries the good in you.

INSTRUCTIONS ON LISTENING TO THE TREES

BY MAHOGANY L. BROWNE

When you are part of a community
You have to think about others

Think about the sun
And how it smiles sweet authority
Think about the ecosystem
And how the leaves dress the tree trunks
Surviving from the kindness of the sun
Yes, the sun and trees have a community all their own

And aren't we part of their community, too?
Benefiting from the oxygen and water, it creates new life
The water is alive in its gift giving
Think of how it feeds the roots

Like any true community
We must nourish and care for one another
If we are to grow

So I listen to the trees when the wind dances near
And I listen to the neighbor's dog singing to the moon
The moon is high because of the water
How amazing!

And this is when I remember home
the way my friends ring the doorbell to come outside and play
the way a car slows down when a ball rolls in its way
the way we make jokes about the TV show and share our fears
the way we look up sadly when the streetlights come on

We all are part of someone else's journey
That's the way communities are built
Each root sprawling toward the edge of an infinite smile

I'VE BEEN THERE BEFORE

BY OLIVIA GATWOOD

when a person is in pain
sometimes the best cure
is to hear *i've felt that too*
from someone else.
when you cry and your best friend
puts their hand on your shoulder and
says, *i've been there before*
suddenly, you know you are not the only one.
sometimes, we don't know the people
we feel for. sometimes, we've never been
where they are. but we don't need
to look like each other or speak like each other
or live like each other to know what it feels
like to be sad, to be hurt, to be in need of a friend.
instead, we can simply say the words
i understand, we can make a secret club
out of our sadness, we can let everyone in
who wants to join, we can sit in a circle
and laugh and share, sing over and over
you are not alone.

WHAT'S IN A NAME?

BY MAHOGANY L. BROWNE

if you are denied a job
because of your height
or your educational background
because of your skin color
or the enunciation of your name

if you are denied a place to live
because of your religion
or your loved ones
because of your musical taste
or your choice of clothes

if you are denied the right to safe passage
to walk freely without harm into a record store
or a pharmacy

remember those who came before us
they did not go quietly
they sat at the lunch counters for everyone's
right to service
they endured brutalities from water hoses and dog bites
to ensure our humanity was respected

they set into motion the lighthouse
shining a path to a brighter possibility
and it is up to us to follow the sharp beams of truth
until our country celebrates with equal fervor
our families' names

GIFT OF GRACE
BY MAHOGANY L. BROWNE

Forgive me
The most lonely request I know

It requires the gift
of grace

Like a horse looping around Central Park
slow and metered

The wind can tell when the body is holding more
weight than it can hold

This is how an apology begins
The bags holstered to the back
across the shoulders
and the neck

The heaviness of disappointment
The sadness is so lonely

        alone and alone

sometimes the wind picks up speed
sometimes the sky is still howling
sometimes you have to wait for the quiet of the
rain
let the storm pass
and try again

I'm sorry
I made a mistake

Forgive me
A humble request
Such a beautiful song

SAY THE NAMES
BY ELIZABETH ACEVEDO

Say the names
of leaders who came before
and made the world better;
say their names,
so that uttering letters
might lend you courage.

Say the name:

Malcolm X.
Cesar Chavez.
Liliuokalani.

Say the name:

Ida B. Wells.
Sonia Sotomayor.
Mamá Tingó.

Say the name:

Malala Yousafzai.
Frida Kahlo.
Colin Kaepernick.

Say the name:

Frederick Douglass.
Sojourner Truth.
Tarana Burke.

Say the name:

Harvey Milk.
Janet Mock.
Audre Lorde.

Say the names
of these leaders
who fought with words
that landed like right hooks;

these leaders who took a stand

so they could assert the dignity of fair pay,
so girls would be treated equally,
so their homes would be respected,
so they could protect the right to protest,
so they could promote racial justice
and the right to love who you love;
be who you are—

And know it doesn't matter your age,
or where you come from:
If you see someone hurt, or down,
if you feel like your community is being cheated or wronged,
instead of stepping over someone fallen
or thinking this is just the way it has to be,
use whatever power you have
to help lift them up   to lift them out.
to lift yourself up   to lift yourself out.
Because freedom isn't freedom
unless it's freedom for us all
So say the names of your heroes
and then say your name, too;
be inspired by the freedom fighters
who have come before
and the justice seeker inside of you.

IN BETWEEN, THERE IS LIGHT
BY OLIVIA GATWOOD

Imagine a rainbow.
Now imagine a rainbow without just seven colors,
but hundreds of colors, the lights and darks
of every shade—neon colors, in-between colors,
colors you're not sure what to call—
Now imagine that someone points to this rainbow
and says, "There are only two colors!"
Imagine that this person says that one color
is a boy and the other is a girl.
What would you say? Maybe you would run your hand
along it like a river, point to all of the
hues and tones, maybe you would ask,
"How can you say that? Look at how many there are!"

The truth is, there are so many shades between boy and girl—
People who are neither, people who are both, people
who live somewhere in the middle. We don't have to choose.
We can just be. And if someone pointed at one part of
the rainbow and said, "This color is better than all of
the others," what would you say?
Maybe you would run your hand along it like a piano,
play a little song with every unique note.
Maybe you would ask, "How can you say that? Listen
to the song they play together!"
Sometimes, the world wants one color of the rainbow
to be louder than the rest, stronger
than the rest, bigger than the rest. Do you know what I tell them?
I say, "Look up, into the sky, do you see it? Look how
perfect it is as a whole."

UNFURLING PEOPLE
BY ELIZABETH ACEVEDO

People leave their homes
even when they love their homes
because people are like flowers:
and sometimes, the places where we live
do not have enough to water us all,
or they have enough sunlight,
but it's being used to scorch us;
or the soil is fertile, but those who tend it
want to pluck us straight out
before we've grown to our full potential.
And so, immigration is like tucking your roots
carefully into yourself
and repotting in a different land.

Immigration is an attempt to
bloom and blossom
and brighten a new place
with the colors and scents
you've brought with you.
It is an attempt to remember
where you are from, and the place that made you,
and also unfurl to the possibilities
of the new place you call home.

Immigration is learning to stretch
into a bridge,
backward and forward,
one limb in each place,
learning to hold tight to traditions
and customs and names and memories in one hand,
and with the other hand let go and lean in
to a place you hope will see you
for all the beauty that you bring.

WHAT IS AN INTERSECTION?

BY MAHOGANY L. BROWNE
AND OLIVIA GATWOOD

An intersection is a place
where things come together—
like four cars waiting
to go different directions
at a stoplight.

People intersect too
not just while moving down the street
but in who we are—
inside our bodies is a
stoplight where our identities come together
to make us a house of flamethrowers
to make us a river of living things.

We all have multiple identities—
you might be in a room full of girls,
but no two are exactly alike—

Classmate with nose ring and printed headband
Soccer player with flowing scarf and full smile
Student in library with brown skin and headphones
Skateboarder with hat to the back and book in hand
Swimmer with painted nails and crew cut
Dancer who says, "Only call me by my name."

That's intersectionality.
We all have different experiences of the world.
And we all have experiences we share.

Intersectionality means
paths crossing one another with respect.

Intersectionality means
moving with intentionality and
acknowledgment of your surroundings.

Intersectionality means
we are all happening, we are all supporting
each other.

We are an ecosystem, living and growing,
depending on each other for survival,
evolving and becoming whole.

TEETH DANCE WITH SILVER

BY MAHOGANY L. BROWNE

Eliza is dressed uniquely
like a mannequin from three different stores
She wears a red dress
with pink leggings underneath
She wears a yellow sneaker on her right foot
and a white sneaker on her left foot
Her socks have bumblebees dancing on them
and touch her knees
She sports candy pop rings on both of her thumbs
She wears a scarf the color of grass
and her teeth dance with silver

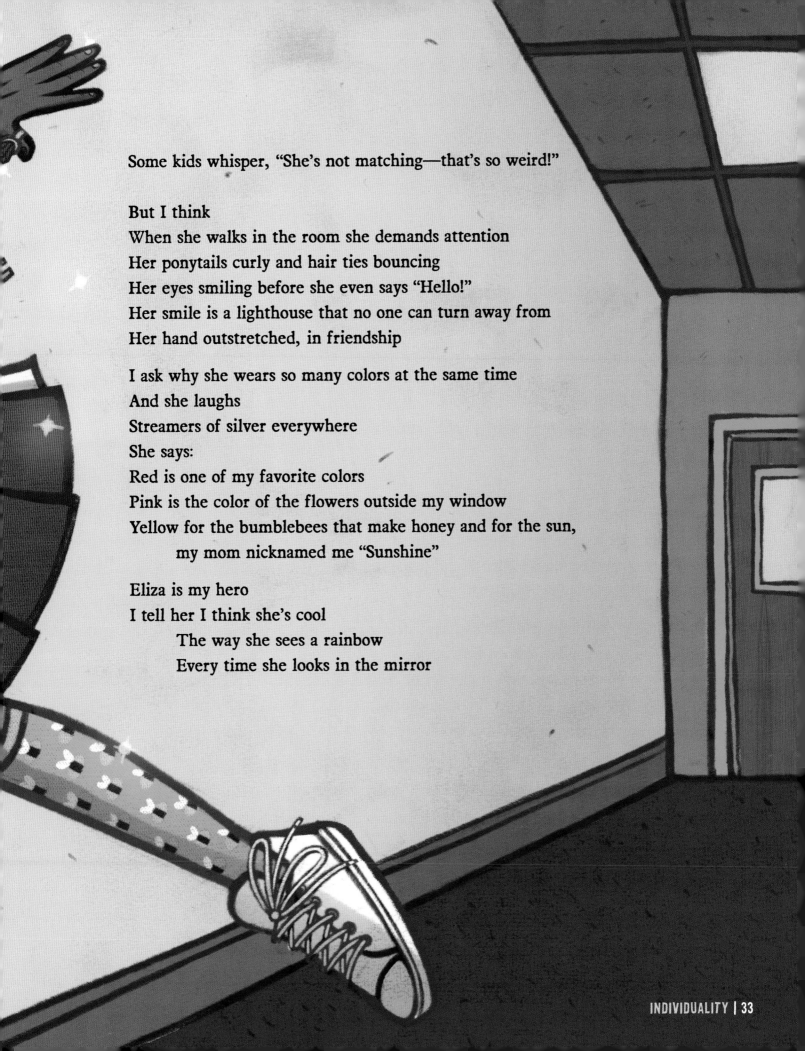

Some kids whisper, "She's not matching—that's so weird!"

But I think
When she walks in the room she demands attention
Her ponytails curly and hair ties bouncing
Her eyes smiling before she even says "Hello!"
Her smile is a lighthouse that no one can turn away from
Her hand outstretched, in friendship

I ask why she wears so many colors at the same time
And she laughs
Streamers of silver everywhere
She says:
Red is one of my favorite colors
Pink is the color of the flowers outside my window
Yellow for the bumblebees that make honey and for the sun,
          my mom nicknamed me "Sunshine"

Eliza is my hero
I tell her I think she's cool
          The way she sees a rainbow
          Every time she looks in the mirror

ORCHARD OF WE

BY MAHOGANY L. BROWNE

From blossoms we arrived like a fruit waiting to be chosen
a ripened joy in the bins at a grocery store
a relocation of home

From the orchard our hands clasped together
and we eat the meat closest to the pit

Peel the bananas and mangoes with a swift hand
bend our heads back in laughter

From the market   our hands clasped together
and we share the fruit of the fruit
find a bowl to hold our bounty, use a spoon to spread
the heap

Sweet fruit
Sweeter family
The summer is a farmers market on repeat
Laughter crowds the atmosphere and lands neatly
on our cheeks

Peaches and watermelon rinds and kiwi dreams
waves crashing against our eyelids in glee
to become what we love with our eyes open and bellies full
to be an orchard living among so many orchards
to blossom and become this impossible joy

BLOWN-OUT STARS WHISPER ABOUT JUSTICE

BY MAHOGANY L. BROWNE

What if the crowd were a forest?
How would you keep it from catching on fire?

Tonight,
the horizon is lit up
like the brightest bulb

The town sits beneath the blown-out stars

The town vibrates with a nameless sound

But the wind remembers their names

And someone somewhere whispers "injustice"

Right then,
the flames grow legs and arms and hands with a booming heartbeat

Now remember the forest?
Can you see the crowd?

The young wildling
The necessary weeds
The patch of wildflowers scattered
The manicured brush
of lush and wilting leaves growing growing growing

What if the sky rained?
What if all the forest of people needed was water?

What if all the breathing bodies required to live
and thrive and graze and grow in harmony
                                        was justice?

AMARI EXPLAINS A FROWN TO HER LITTLE BROTHER

BY MAHOGANY L. BROWNE

When my friends walk through the convenience
store
Almost always
Someone follows them

It's like a shadow of distrust
Looming above their bronze skin
They say it's 'cause we look different

When my babysitter walks through the store
No one ever follows her

It's like a cloud of light
guides her path through each aisle
She says she probably reminds them of the mother
from old black-and-white TV shows

When I try to explain to my little brother
What it means to be judged
What it means to be ignored
What it means to be silenced

I can only think of *Brown v. Board*
I can only think of Jim Crow
I can only think of the 13th Amendment

My little brother is too young to understand the
13th Amendment abolished slavery and involuntary
servitude in the United States

But my little brother knows what a smile means
And my little brother knows what a hug means
And my little brother knows what a friend is

When we go to the park with our babysitter

and I watch the clouds move above his curly curly hair
I feel like anything is possible

I try to explain to my little brother
What I learned in history class
And why I'm so sad and I want to tell him

About Jordan Davis or Trayvon Martin or Emmett Till
stories from long ago and just yesterday
that I read about people who look like us
and our friends and our neighbors
But he grabs my hand and squeezes
because the words get caught in the tears
threatening to run from my eyes
I just want to cry
Because my brother is my little brother
He's my favorite person and he doesn't
care about how different I may look
Just that I'm as beautiful and friendly as our grandmother
And I'm as kind and curious as our grandfather

So instead I lead him to the squeaky swing set
And think I'll wait another day to explain to him
what it means when someone doesn't like you
without ever saying hello

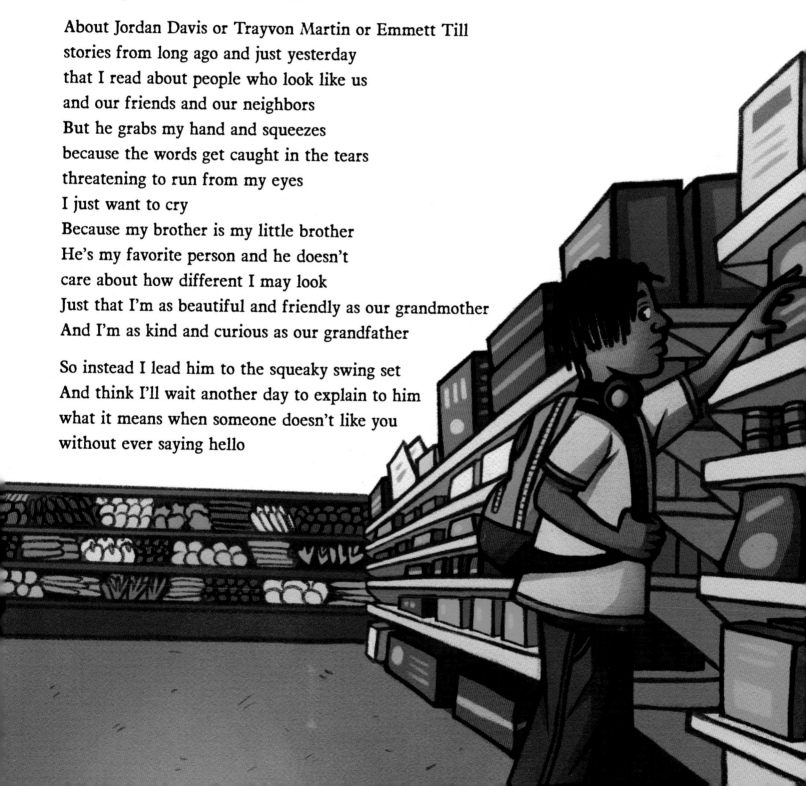

WHAT'S IN MY TOOLBOX?
BY OLIVIA GATWOOD

We can't choose the way we're born.
Some of us are born with two parents, some one, some none.
Some of us are born with legs that we can walk with,
some of us need a little help. Some of us get to eat when
we are hungry, some of us still haven't. When a person
has privilege, it is a toolbox they were born with,
hammers and nails that make it easier for them
to walk through the world because the world,
in all of its beauty and excitement and variety,
can still be a very hard place in which to live.
Privilege makes it feel easier for some people—
a white person can walk down the street
and not worry about being discriminated against
while a person of color cannot.
Our friends might have a toolbox filled with gadgets
we wish we had, or we might have gizmos we didn't
even know others don't have. And even though
it's true we don't choose privilege, we still have
the toolbox with us all the time.
We can choose to keep the tools for ourselves, or we can choose
to use it to help people who don't have what we do.
We can ask our parents to pick our friends up from practice
if they don't have a ride, we can tell our school we need
more ramps for kids on wheels, we can invite friends
over for dinner and send them off with a full belly.
Privilege might make it easier for one person
to build the house, but that doesn't mean
they should build it just for themselves.
If we have privilege, we must listen.
When we understand each other, we can build a house that fits everyone.
We can use our tools to build the house together.
In this house, the door is always open—
Come in.

RIGHT TO
AFTER CLAUDE MCKAY
BY MAHOGANY L. BROWNE

If we must live, let it not be in silence
Each shadow surrounding our right to be outraged
Let us not sit hands crossed while our stomachs growl upset
Full of bad food and assembly-line ideas
Listen closely: our bodies bubbling up angrily at the lies
we have been fed

If we must live, let no one decide how our hearts beat
Or how our songs should be sung
Or if our neighborhoods are worth protecting
Or if we are allowed to walk in stores freely

If we must live, let it be a true life
One full of choices and opportunities
One that isn't designed to push us into a corner
Keep us quiet and formidable
Keep us without unique opinions and educated understandings

If we must live—
And we must—
Let it be with our fists in the air
To remind the people that we will speak up
for what is right
We will always stand up against that which brings harm
We will demand what is just
Not only for our own lives
but for the lives that are impacted
by injustice

Let us live
to fight for a better day
every day
for everyone.

ROCK THE BOAT

BY ELIZABETH ACEVEDO

Someone might tell you,
"Don't rock the boat"
when they want you to hush.
When they are afraid of change.
When they are doing something wrong
or that makes them ashamed and they don't
want anyone to know.

There is a feeling you might get
when they say that,
when you know someone has done
or said something unjust. Something
that might hurt you or another being.

That feeling might be a tightening in your chest.
Or a tightening of your fists.
And most times you should not thrust out either
but you should follow that feeling and speak up
and speak out.

Even if it doesn't feel easy,
Rock the boat. Rock the boat.

Practice saying "Don't do that to her."
or "You're hurting him."
or "I don't feel good when you . . ."

Speaking up might make your hands shake,
or your voice small,
or your heart flutter like a bird taking flight,
that feeling, the tightening in your chest,
or the tightening of your fists—you may not have to thrust out either—
but trust that your body is telling you to speak up and speak out

because even if it doesn't feel easy,
Rock the boat. Rock the boat.

And sometimes it might seem you are the only one
who can see or feel that something is not quite right
in how another is being treated,
or in how you are being treated,

and you may want to be quiet
so as not to rock the boat,

but just know
you contain waves,
you are an ocean,
your heart is as large as lakes
and when it quakes
you have to rise,
and rise, and let the tide inside you
shake every single ship
that would attempt to sweep
someone beneath:

Rock the boat, rock the boat,
with love and hope, rock the boat.

WE MAKE A FIST
BY MAHOGANY L. BROWNE

The girl up the block is good at coloring in the lines

The kid next door is great at popping wheelies

My cousin across the street is a magician when it comes to making songs

And my brother is good at baking cookies

When we want to have a picnic
We bring our greatest talents
Put them all on the blanket
And share with each other
The laughter and songs
The artwork and baked goods
Created by our hands

THE POET'S PEN

BY MAHOGANY L. BROWNE

What does the silence of a people sound like?
Maybe:
The silence you hold in your chest
  The silence before a body falls to the ground
  The silence after a cry pierces the air
  The silence when listening for a newborn's breath

Or   does it sound like an orchid growing toward the sun?
    does it sound like a moon moving above the crashing waters?
    does it sound like a poet and the poet's pen?

  Moving against the paper
  speaking stories about their home city
and a single mother's song.

Moving against the paper
speaking stories about farming
and a father's well-wishes
or a graduation ceremony.

Moving against the paper
speaking stories about bicycle spokes
and trading cards clicking hello to passersby.

A silence can sound like many things.
That is why we choose to write
poems as a people's almanac
for those unable to speak.

A ME-SHAPED BOX

BY OLIVIA GATWOOD

We live in a world that likes boxes—
boxy houses, boxy cars,
cardboard boxes & mailboxes
& shoeboxes too
& in those boxes we put our things
& our families & letters
to our friends across the world.

But we also have imaginary boxes—
boxes where we put people
based on what we've learned
from our families
or what we see on TV.

Before we even know someone,
we say, "If you look like that,
you go in this box!"
Or, "If you talk like this,
you go in that box!"

Stereotyping is all of the little boxes
in our heads that insist
on fitting people, with all of their
different shapes and sizes and colors
and voices, into a home they didn't build
for themselves.

Stereotyping keeps us
from getting to know people
for who they are.
Stereotyping makes other people
feel like they aren't individuals.

So resist the box!
Burn it down!
Why have a box
when we could have a swimming pool
or a trampoline park?
A playground or a giant green field?
We don't need those silly squares!
We need to let everyone be
exactly the way they are
so that we can be too.
And isn't that so much better
than a boring old box?

WE CARRY OUR ROOTS

BY MAHOGANY L. BROWNE AND ELIZABETH ACEVEDO

On Friday nights, the mothers of my church
arm themselves in prayer and weave hope together
like wreaths of flowers placed on the doors
of sick people at the hospital who have no one to visit them.

On the first Saturday of the month,
my cousin grabs a book from the bookstore shelves.
Little kids gather around, claim their seat on the carpet.
Eyes beam bright lights as he begins to read out loud.

On Tuesdays, my best friend shakes off tiredness,
even when it cloaks him like a coat. He sits
across kids who struggle with a subject he is great at: math.
He is patient and watchful as he helps them understand.

During winter break, we beeline assembly style
at the shelter. We ignore the icy rings around our breath.
We spoon soup into bowls until the pot is empty
and return to the church's kitchen to grab another offering.

Ready to begin again.
We don't serve for an award we believe we deserve.
We use our hands and our words knowing the seeds will emerge.
We may not see the fruit, but we carry the roots

we move forward   every time we give back.

WOKE

BY MAHOGANY L. BROWNE

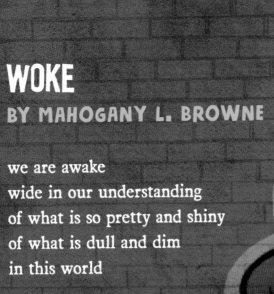

we are awake
wide in our understanding
of what is so pretty and shiny
of what is dull and dim
in this world

but look here

even wider
between our outstretched arms
a brave and growing world

look closely

don't forget
we invited you here
to live inside
this truth
this freedom

we never sleep on what's at stake

ABOUT THE AUTHORS

MAHOGANY L. BROWNE is a writer, an organizer, and an educator. She is the author of several poetry collections for adults, including *Kissing Caskets* and *#Dear Twitter*. Her books for children and teenagers include *Black Girl Magic* and *Woke Baby*, the companion book to *Woke*. She is the artistic director of Urban Word NYC and has received literary fellowships from Agnes Gund, AIR Serenbe, Cave Canem, Poets House, and the Robert Rauschenberg Foundation. She lives in Brooklyn, New York. mobrowne.com

ELIZABETH ACEVEDO is the *New York Times*—bestselling author of *The Poet X* and *With the Fire On High*. She is a winner of the National Book Award for Young People's Literature, the Michael L. Printz Award, the Pura Belpré Award, the Boston Globe—Horn Book Award, and the Walter Dean Myers Award for Outstanding Children's Literature. She is a National Poetry Slam champion and holds an MFA in creative writing from the University of Maryland. She lives in Washington, DC, with her partner. acevedowrites.com

OLIVIA GATWOOD has received international recognition for her poetry, performances, and work as an educator in sexual assault prevention and recovery. She is the author of the poetry chapbook *New American Best Friend* and has had her work featured on MTV, HBO, and BBC, among others. Her poems have appeared in such publications as *Muzzle*, *Winter Tangerine*, *Poetry City*, *Tinderbox Poetry Journal*, and *The Missouri Review*. She is from Albuquerque, New Mexico. oliviagatwood.com

These poems are for the young poets righting the wrongs and braving the stage fearlessly. Shout-out to Urban Word NYC and the many after-school programs providing safe passage for our young literary heroes. Keep scribing. We need you. —M.B.

For the world makers to whom I offer all my hopes: Zaria, Aria, and Yara —E.A.

For Eli —O.G.

To my mother, Leslie, for teaching me the power of the written word —T.T.

Foreword copyright © 2020 by Jason Reynolds
Introduction copyright © 2020 by Mahogany L. Browne
"Activism, Everywhere," "The Ability to Be," "In the Next," "Instructions on Listening to the Trees," "What's in a Name?," "Gift of Grace,"
"Teeth Dance with Silver," "Orchard of We," "Blown-Out Stars Whisper about Justice," "Amari Explains a Frown to Her Little Brother,"
"Right To," "We Make a Fist," "The Poet's Pen," "Woke" © 2020 by Mahogany L. Browne
"The Good Body," "Say the Names," "Unfurling People," "Rock the Boat" © 2020 by Elizabeth Acevedo
"I've Been There Before," "In Between, There Is Light," "What's in My Toolbox?," "A Me-Shaped Box" © 2020 by Olivia Gatwood
"What Is an Intersection?" © 2020 by Mahogany L. Browne and Olivia Gatwood
"We Carry Our Roots" © 2020 by Mahogany L. Browne and Elizabeth Acevedo
Illustrations copyright © 2020 by Theodore Taylor III
Published by Roaring Brook Press
Roaring Brook Press is a division of Holtzbrinck Publishing Holdings Limited Partnership
120 Broadway, New York, NY 10271
mackids.com

Library of Congress Control Number: 2019941024
ISBN: 978-1-250-31120-7

Our books may be purchased in bulk for promotional, educational, or business use. Please contact your local bookseller or the Macmillan Corporate and Premium Sales Department at (800) 221-7945 ext. 5442 or by email at MacmillanSpecialMarkets@macmillan.com.

First edition, 2020
Book design by Monique Sterling
Printed in China by RR Donnelley Asia Printing Solutions Ltd.,
Dongguan City, Guangdong Province

1 3 5 7 9 10 8 6 4 2